This storybook belongs to

....

First published in Great Britain 2022 by Farshore
An imprint of HarperCollins*Publishers*
1 London Bridge Street, London SE1 9GF
www.farshore.co.uk

HarperCollins*Publishers*
1st Floor, Watermarque Building, Ringsend Road
Dublin 4, Ireland

ISBN 978 0 7555 0399 5
Printed in Great Britain by Bell and Bain Ltd, Glasgow
001

A CIP catalogue record for this title is available from the British Library.

MIX
Paper from
responsible sources
FSC
www.fsc.org
FSC® C007454

COUNT ON THE EASTER PUPS!

It's almost time for the Adventure Bay Easter Egg Hunt.
"You can count on the PAW Patrol and our friends to get things ready," says Ryder.

Rocky finds **ONE** big basket.

"Don't lose it – reuse it!" he says.

Tracker and Mayor Goodway make **TWO** beautiful bows.

"This will be the best egg hunt ever," says the mayor.

Marshall and Everest water **THREE** big, colourful flowers. "We're ruff-ruff ready for the egg hunt!" says Marshall.

Rubble plays with **FOUR** hopping friends.
"You can't have an Easter party without adorable bunnies,"
he says with a giggle.

Mr Porter shares **FIVE** bags of yummy jelly beans.

Chase sniffs **SIX** sweet treats.

Rocky has **SEVEN** bowls of bright dye.
"I'm egg-cited to start decorating!" he says.

EIGHT pups do the perfect Easter dance – the bunny hop!

Skye hangs **NINE** fluttering flags.

"This party is about to take off!" she says.

"There are **TEN** eggs hidden here," says Ryder. "Let's find them all!"

It's time for an Easter Hunt

These items are hidden throughout this book. Go back to the beginning and see if you can spot them.

A bunny with a bow

A basket of bunnies

A tree with a big bow

A black and white flag

A bunny rabbit

A pink flower in a pot

A cupcake with a cherry

A trolley filled with eggs

THE END

A SNUGGLY, SNOOZY, BEDTIME STORYBOOK

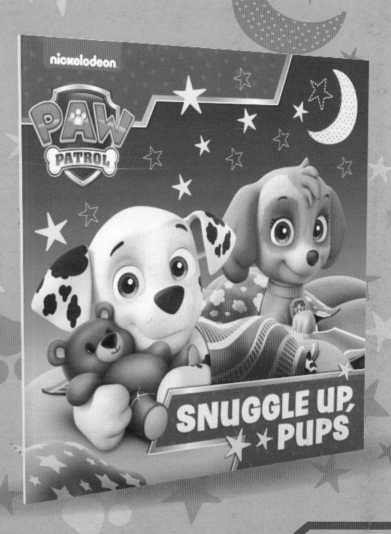

Join the sleepy **PAW patrol** puppies as they get cosy
and say **goodnight** to the team. **Snuggle up, Pups!**

ISBN: 978-0-7555-0267-7

A ROARSOME DINOSAUR STICKER ACTIVITY BOOK

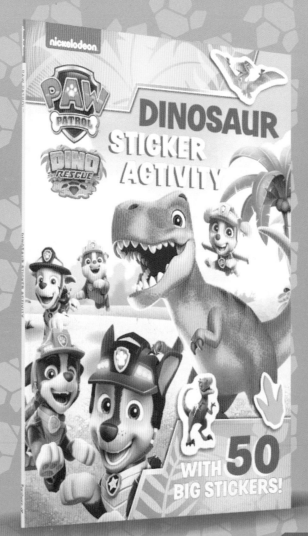

Join the **PAW Patrol** on their **dino adventures!** Enjoy the **fun activities** and **BIG stickers** with your favourite pups and their dinosaur friends.

ISBN: 978-0-7555-0424-4